W9-AMB-588

Dear mouse friends,
Welcome to the world of

Geronimo Stilton

The Editorial Staff of
The Rodent's Gazette

1. Linda Thinslice
2. Sweetie Cheesetriangle
3. Ratella Redfur
4. Soya Mousehao
5. Cheesita de la Pampa
6. Mouseanna Mousetti
7. Yale Youngmouse
8. Toni Tinypaw
9. Tina Spicytail
10. William Shortpaws
11. Valerie Vole
12. Trap Stilton
13. Branwen Musclemouse
14. Zeppola Zap
15. Merenguita Gingermouse
16. Ratsy O'Shea
17. Rodentrick Roundrat
18. Teddy von Muffler
19. Thea Stilton
20. Erronea Misprint
21. Pinky Pick
22. Ya-ya O'Cheddar
23. Mousella MacMouser
24. Kreamy O'Cheddar
25. Blasco Tabasco
26. Toffie Sugarsweet
27. Tylerat Truemouse
28. Larry Keys
29. Michael Mouse
30. Geronimo Stilton
31. Benjamin Stilton
32. Briette Finerat
33. Raclette Finerat

Geronimo Stilton
A learned and brainy
mouse; editor of
The Rodent's Gazette

Thea Stilton
Geronimo's sister and
special correspondent at
The Rodent's Gazette

Trap Stilton
An awful joker;
Geronimo's cousin and
owner of the store
Cheap Junk for Less

Benjamin Stilton
A sweet and loving
nine-year-old mouse;
Geronimo's favorite
nephew

Geronimo Stilton

IT'S HALLOWEEN, YOU 'FRAIDY MOUSE!

Scholastic Inc.

New York   Toronto   London   Auckland   Sydney
Mexico City   New Delhi   Hong Kong   Buenos Aires

ISBN 978-0-439-55973-7

Based on an original idea by Elisabetta Dami.

www.geronimostilton.com

Published by Scholastic Inc., 557 Broadway, New York, NY 10012. SCHOLASTIC and associated logos are trademarks and/or registered trademarks of Scholastic Inc.

Stilton is the name of a famous English cheese. It is a registered trademark of the Stilton Cheese Makers' Association. For more information, go to www.stiltoncheese.com.

Text by Geronimo Stilton
Original title *Halloween . . . che fifa felina!*
Cover by Matt Wolf, revised by Larry Keys
Graphics by Merenguita Gingermouse and Marina Bonanni

Special thanks to Kathryn Cristaldi
Translated by Joan L. Giurdanella
Interior design by Kay Petronio

29 28 27 26 25 24 23   12 13 14 15 16/0

Printed in the U.S.A.   40
First printing, September 2004

SEE, THERE'S NOTHING THERE . . .

It was a rainy October night. I was working late at the office.

The only sound was coming from the rain outside my window.

DRIP, DRIP, DRIP . . .

It was so peaceful. So soothing. Smiling, I casually glanced out the window. Cheese niblets! A GHOST was staring right back at me!

I JUMPED to my paws. Squeak!! My

whiskers began trembling with fear. *Get a grip, Geronimo*, I told myself.

I cleaned my glasses. When I looked again, the ghost was gone.

"See, there's nothing there," I said out loud.

I stared down at the book I had been reading. The words swam before my eyes. *I must be tired*, I decided. Maybe it was time to go home.

But just then, the lights went out! What was going on? I yanked open my desk drawer. I had to find my flashlight. Suddenly, I spotted something glowing at the bottom of the drawer. What was it?

I stretched out my paw and touched . . . a skull! Rancid rat hairs! I jumped so high, my fur touched the ceiling.

I raced to the door. I grabbed the doorknob. It felt STICKY. How strange.

Brrrrrrrrrrrrrrrrrr

I opened my desk drawer and . . .

The cleaning mice were usually so careful. Maybe I should squeak with them.

But there was no time to worry about it now. I raised my paw up to the moonlight to get a better look. What was that dripping from my fur? It was sticky. It was red. It was **BLOOD!**

I felt faint. The sight of blood does that to me. My heart was racing like a speed skater at the Mouse Olympics.

I ran down the **DARK HALL**, squeaking at the top of my lungs.

All of a sudden, a white shape peeped out from around the corner. *"Boo!"* it howled.

My jaw hit the ground. I started to sweat. I was so scared, I could hardly breathe. I felt like I was starring in a terrifying horror-mouse movie! Do you like horror movies? I hate them. Especially the ones where the mouse is home alone and the phone rings. The caller says he's coming after the mouse. Then the mouse runs around in circles, squeaking and pulling

5

out his fur. They're the worst. I spend half the movie with my paws covering my eyes.

I chewed my whiskers. Just thinking about those movies made me shake. I rushed toward the office lobby. I had to get out. I had to get away.

At last, I reached the front door. But it was locked. Someone or something had locked me in!

Meoooowwwwwwwwwwwwwww!!!

"HELP!" I squeaked, rattling the knob.

At first, there was

6

silence. Then I heard a sound. Yes, someone was on the other side of the door. Cheesecake! I was saved! Maybe it was Fuzzy, the night watchmouse. Fuzzy was an older rodent. His eyes were kind of going. And his ears were shot. But I just couldn't bring myself to fire him. How could I? He was such a sweet, kind, gentle rodent. Yes, they just don't make them like Fuzzy anymore. Now I couldn't wait to see his friendly snout.

But instead of seeing good, old

hideous skeleton

Fuzzy, I heard a horrifying sound.

"Meooooowwwwwwwwwwww!"

It was a CAT! Terrified, I turned around and ran. I had to reach the emergency exit. I could just make out the glow-in-the-dark sign up ahead. But something else was glowing next to it. What was it? I squinted my eyes to see better. That's when my paws screeched to a halt. A hideous, gleaming white skeleton stared back at me.

"Hi, Gerrybaby! **Trick** or **treat**?" the skeleton sneered.

I blinked. I knew that voice. Yes, I knew it very well. It was my annoying cousin Trap.

At that moment, the lights flicked back on. A familiar snout appeared before me.

"Gerrykins, my mouse!" Trap smirked. "You're so easy to SCARE."

Y-Y-Y-Y-Y-You!
Y-Y-Y-Y-Y-You!

I was so mad, I lost my squeak.

I shook my paw in the air. I pounded my tail on the ground. My snout turned red with rage. "Y-Y-Y-Y-Y-You! Y-Y-Y-Y-Y-You!" I finally managed to stutter.

My cousin just giggled with glee. He shook his paw in the air. "Y-Y-Y-Y-Y-You!" he sneered, making fun of me.

I chewed my whiskers. STEAM poured out of my ears. Have I told you my cousin is the most annoying mouse on the planet? He

is loud. He is rude. And he loves to play tricks. Especially on me.

Now Trap pinched my tail. "You had to see your face when you saw the skull

in your desk drawer!" he hooted. "You're such a **SCAREDY MOUSE**, Cousinkins!"

Then he pulled a notepad out of his pocket. Deep in thought, he began to **scribble** on it. "Let's see," he mumbled. "I'll give the little skull a 10. I'll give the fake blood on the doorknob a 9. The skeleton gets an 8½. But the ghost needs work. It wasn't scary enough."

What was my cousin babbling about? Well, it turns out he had started working with his friend Paws Prankster. Paws had opened a store called Tricks for Tails. It was filled with gag gifts, magic tricks, and practical jokes. Trap's job was to test out some of the Halloween stuff.

"Don't you just love HALLOWEEN, Germeister?" he snickered. "I can't wait for October 31!"

I rolled my eyes. "I can't wait to get home," I grumbled.

I left, slamming the door behind me. The truth is, I hate Halloween. I hate scary parties. I hate scary costumes. And I especially hate scary candy. What's scary candy? Moldy cheese, of course. Last year, my next-door neighbor gave out moldy Cheesy Chews to every trick-or-treater. Now, *that's* frightening!

PAWS AS COLD AS ICE

I started walking home. Luckily, my mouse hole is only a few blocks from *The Rodent's Gazette.* What is *The Rodent's Gazette*? Oops, silly me. I completely forgot to introduce myself. My name is Stilton, *Geronimo Stilton*. I am a writer and the publisher of *The Rodent's Gazette.* It is the best newspaper on **Mouse Island.**

Now, let's see, where was I? Ah, yes, I was headed back home. When I got there, I pulled out my key to open the door. Just then, two paws as cold as ice covered my eyes.

"Heeeeellllppppp!

Don't hurt me!" I squeaked in terror.

"You can have anything you want. Take my watch! Take my coat! Take my firstborn rodent!"

My attacker uncovered my eyes. It was only my sister, Thea. "Crispy cheese crackers! Pull yourself together, Gerry Berry!" she scolded. "It's just me. What a scaredy mouse!"

I had turned as WHITE as a piece of mozzarella. I was breathing hard. Why did my family insist on playing pranks on me? They knew I hated surprises. They knew I hated to be scared.

I tried to pry open the door, but my sister blocked my way. "Not so fast, Germeister," she squeaked. "I came to talk to you about Halloween."

Ugh. There it was again. HALLOWEEN.

Why do mice love Halloween? It's such a spooky holiday. Just thinking about October 31 makes my fur stand on end.

I tried to tune her out, but my sister kept squeaking away. She said she had a great idea. She thought we should publish a book about HALLOWEEN. It would have everything you need to plan a party: spooky party games, costume ideas, and even terrifying recipes.

"It will sell like hot cheese cider at the Furtown Fall Festival!" she insisted. "The only problem is, we will have to publish it RIGHT AWAY."

I nodded. After all, no one wants to read a Halloween book after the holiday is over. And Halloween was only a week away.

But who would be able to write a book that fast? I tapped my head with my paw.

Think, think, think, I told myself. Just then, I noticed my sister was staring at me. She grinned. Uh-oh. I knew that look. It meant she had an idea. Thea's ideas can be scary. Once, she decided I needed some spice in my life. She took me hang gliding. I fell out of the glider and ended up in a prickly bush. I still have nightmares about it.

Thea winked at me. "You're a writer, big brother," she declared. "You can write the book about Halloween. You'll just have to work fast. You have twenty-four hours."

I held up my paws. "Oh, no, not **me**!" I shrieked. "I hate Halloween! And I don't know anything about parties or costumes!" *No way,* I told myself. I would never write a book about a holiday I hated.

Of course, my sister wouldn't give up. Once she gets an idea in her head, there's no stopping her. She's like the Rodents Express train. Full speed ahead!

She said I could get help from my cousin. "Trap knows a lot about scary tricks and stuff now that he's working at **Tricks for Tails**," she explained.

I rolled my eyes. There was no way that I would ever ask my cousin for advice. His ideas were scarier than my sister's.

"Forget it," I declared, stamping my paw. "I, *Geronimo Stilton*, will never do it. **No**, make that **never, ever**," I added.

Then I dashed into my mouse hole and slammed the door before Thea could stop me. What a horrible **niGHt**.

BURT AND SQUEAKER'S CHUNKY CHEDDAR

I hung up my coat. I was tired, cold, and hungry. Maybe a yummy bite to eat would pick up my spirits. I headed for the kitchen.

I opened the refrigerator. It was filled with my favorite food — cheese! I licked my whiskers.

I started off with a double-decker grilled cheese on whole wheat. It was so good, I **nibbled** it down in four bites. Next, I opened the freezer. I pulled out a tub of Burt and Squeaker's Chunky Cheddar. Have you ever tasted Chunky Cheddar? It's one of my favorite cheese-flavored ice creams.

YUM YUM YUM YUM YUM YUM YUM YUM

I started off with a double-decker grilled cheese. . . .

"YUM, YUM!" I said with a sigh.

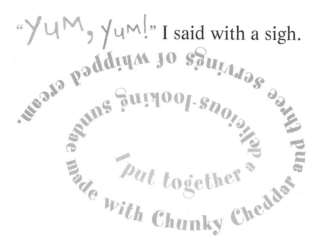

put together a delicious-looking sundae made with Chunky Cheddar and three servings of whipped cream.

I carried my treat into the living room. But then I realized something was wrong. The light was already turned on. Someone was in my mouse hole!

Who could it be? A burglar? A sewer rat? A cat with razor-sharp claws? I shivered. I crept forward on tippy paws.

The fireplace was lit. It filled the room with an eerie glow.

Just then, I saw a *huge shadow* on the wall. It grew taller and taller.

I chewed my whiskers to keep from shrieking. *The shadow was now ten times my size!* Oh, what did it want from me? *Maybe if I don't move, it will leave me alone,* I thought. I froze on the spot. But I was feeling faint. I didn't know how long I could stay still.

All of a sudden, I heard a familiar voice. "Uncle! Uncle Geronimo!" it squeaked.

The shadow grew taller

I looked down. Then I began to giggle. The giant shadow belonged to my little nephew Benjamin! He ran toward me and gave me a hug.

"You left your door open, Uncle," he explained. "I came in to wait for you." Then

and taller!

he looked at me closely. "Uncle, do you feel OK?" he asked. "You look so pale."

I coughed. "Of course, I'm, um, just fine," I told my nephew. Then I smoothed down my fur. I was so **SCARED**, it had been standing on end.

Meanwhile, Benjamin began chattering away happily. He had heard about my sister's idea to write a book on Halloween.

"Can I help you write it?" he pleaded. "We can get some ideas from Uncle Trap's store. It will be so much **fun**. I love Halloween, Uncle! When can we start?"

I sighed. I could never say no to my favorite nephew.

ISN'T IT A SCREAM?

The next morning, we went to the store where Trap worked. Tricks for Tails was a creepy-looking place.

I noticed that the bell was in the shape of a skull. The minute I touched it, I heard a terrifying scream. I jumped so high, my fur brushed the clouds.

The day had just begun, and I was already shaking with fear.

But Benjamin just giggled. "What a neat doorbell!" he said with a grin.

I wiped the sweat from my fur. *Be brave,* I told myself.

AaaaaaaaaghHHHHHHHHHH!!

HEY, YOU! CHEDDARFACE! PRESS HERE!

We went in. The store was **dark** and dusty. And I mean really dusty. It looked like no one had cleaned the place since the Great Cat War! I'm talking fur balls all over the place. I wrinkled my nose.

Then I saw Trap. He was sitting in front of a cash register.

"Hey, there, Cousinkins!" he snickered. "You look a little pale. How do you like the doorbell? Isn't it a scream?"

He pressed a button. The recorded scream made me jump again. My cousin chuckled. "This one is called the *Mummy's SCREAM*," he explained. "But we also have the *Cat's MEOW* and the *Snapping MOUSETRAP*. Do you want to hear them?"

I quickly shook my head to say no. But I said yes when he offered me some candy. After all, my heart was still pounding from

those silly screams. I deserved a little treat.
A nice piece of chocolate would cheer me
right up.

Trap gave me an unopened box. Yum! I
love candy. But when I opened the lid, a
SPRING hit me in the face!

My cousin sneered with satisfaction. "Ha-ha! I knew you would fall for that one!"

I frowned. "So much for a quick pick-me-up," I muttered. It was time to get down to work. I was here to do research. I needed to learn more about scary tricks and party games. Then I could go home and write about them.

At that moment, I spotted a little glass cabinet. It was filled with rubber cheese. I took out a piece of Swiss and squeezed it. The cheese *squeaked*!

Trap took out another piece. "What do you think about this mozzarella? It looks just like the real thing. Go ahead, touch it," he urged.

I did. It felt exactly like a piece of mozzarella. "Cheese

FAKE MOZZARELLA

niblets!" I squeaked. "It even *smells like cheese*! What a perfect fake!"

Trap smirked. "You're right about one thing, Gerry Berry," he said. "It is perfect. But it's not fake." Then he popped the cheese into his mouth. "Tricked you again!" he jeered, his mouth full.

Did I mention my cousin can be a pain in my fur?

Next, Trap led us to a room in the back of the store. The door was shaped like the head of a cat with gaping jaws.

I shivered. The cat looked so real. I could almost hear it hissing at me.

I entered the room with a feeling of dread. It was so dark, I could hardly see my own whiskers. Trap turned on a dim lamp. "Look around if you dare . . ." HE ANNOUNCED IN A SPOOKY VOICE.

Enter if you dare. . . .

I did. A table covered with **CREEPY CRAWLY** insects stood in one corner. A huge cockroach glared at me from the top of the pile. My fur broke out in a sweat. I hate bugs. Once, a mosquito bit me right on my nose. I couldn't smell for a week. I couldn't smell flowers. I couldn't smell the ocean. I couldn't even smell my grandma Onewhisker's stinky blue cheese casseroles!

Just then, an enormous fly buzzed by under my snout. I gasped. Its *red eyes* seemed to glow in the dark.

Zzzzzzzzzzzzzzzz Zzzzzzzzzzzzzzzz Zzzzzzzzzzz

I swatted at the fly. Meanwhile, Trap had picked up an **EVIL-LOOKING** black spider. He hung it on a nail. Then he clapped his paws. The spider raced down a thread

on hairy black legs. Benjamin was thrilled.

"Look, Uncle. It seems so real!" he laughed. He pulled a pad out of his pocket and jotted down a few notes.

"Yes, nephew, it does s-s-seem r-r-real," I stammered. I was trying to stay calm, but these bugs were a bit *too* real for me. I wanted that hairy black spider to go back to its hairy home. I kept my eye on it just in case it wasn't a fake.

Suddenly, Trap shoved something wiggly in front of my face. I screamed. It was a **fat**, **ugly** worm dripping with gray slime.

"Enough, Trap!" I squeaked. "You know I hate bugs!"

My cousin smirked. He was tugging at something under one of the tables. "No problemo, Cuz," he said. "How about we move on to the snakes?" In a flash, he had wrapped a rubber python around my neck.

"Go ahead, scream," Trap told me. But I was one step ahead of him. I was already **SQUEAKING** at the top of my lungs! With every squeak, the rubbery snake grew tighter around my throat. This wasn't a trick. It was torture!

With every squeak, the snake grew tighter...

Benjamin helped peel the disgusting creature off me. Trap just grinned. "Yep, we've got every gross trick in the book here

Aaaaaaaaag HHHHHHHHHHHHHHHHHH!!!!

at **Tricks for Tails**," he declared. "How about I show you our giant cat-skeleton collection?"

I sighed. My nerves were shot. I didn't know how much more I could take. Luckily, we were interrupted by the bell.

Aaaaaaghhhhhhhh!!!!

Trap headed for the door. "A customer. I've got to go!" he squeaked. "You'll have to let yourselves out. Don't let the door hit you in the **tail**."

We left the store. "Uncle Geronimo, maybe we should go check out some costumes next," Benjamin suggested.

I nodded. "Good idea, Nephew," I agreed. Costumes wouldn't be half as scary as Trap's disgusting tricks. I called my assistant

editor, **Pinky Pick**.*
I knew she would be
able to help.

"Boss, I think you
should go visit a friend
of mine," she said. "Her
name is **Creepella von
Cacklefur**. We met at a Halloween
party last year. She had the most
amazing costume. It looked so real.
I'm sure she can help you."

★ Pinky Pick is a fabumouse fourteen-year-old
mouse. Maybe you have already met her....

FABUMOUSE FUNERALS

I jotted down the address of Pinky's friend **Creepella**. Then Benjamin and I jumped in a taxi. Soon we arrived at 33 DARK GRAVE DRIVE.

This place was dark and **spooky**. And it was right next to a cemetery. What a scary place to live! All of those dead mice buried right next door. I wondered if Creepella ever had any ghostly visitors. But there was no time to think about it now. Our taxi pulled up to the house. That's when I noticed a sign on the front lawn.

B. VON CACKLEFUR
Fabumouse Funerals
for the Remarkable Rodent
Group Discounts Available

A hearse was parked in the driveway. Confused, I checked the address. Yes, this was the right place. Could Pinky's friend really live in a funeral parlor?

I rang the bell. A **VERY THIN** mouse all dressed in black came to the door. "Good morning," he croaked in a deep voice. "I am **Boris von Cacklefur**. Which one of you is dead? *Ha-ha-ha, just a joke,*" he cackled.

"Do you need to look at some coffins? I've got a splendid yellow one just in. It looks just like a piece of Swiss. It

33 Dark Grave Drive

even has holes. Not that your mouse will be needing them. *Hee-hee-hee . . .*"

I held up my paw to make him stop. His jokes made me want to run squeaking from the house. "Actually, we're here to see **Creepella von Cacklefur**," I explained.

He looked disappointed. "Oh, so you're not customers; too bad," he murmured. Then he winked. "Still, you will be one day!" he chuckled.

I grew pale. All of this talk about coffins and

Boris 💀 von Cacklefur

death was making my fur crawl.

Boris didn't seem to notice. "Let me get my daughter for you," he went on. "**Creepella**! You have visitors!" he shouted into an intercom.

We started down a hallway, but Boris stopped us. "Not that way!" he called. "That is the way to the morgue. Sorry I can't take you there myself. But I have a customer waiting. Luckily, he's not in a hurry. In fact, he's not even breathing. *Ha-ha-ha!*"

He opened the door and pointed to a path. It wound around through the cemetery.

My fur stood on end.

Oh, what was I doing in this awful place?

My heart was beating like a drum at a Rockin' Rats concert. I wanted to run home with my tail between my paws. But I couldn't. What would my little nephew think? I had to show him I was brave. Or at least that I wasn't a total 'fraidy mouse.

I headed down the path with Benjamin at my side. It was so quiet. So deathly quiet.

Just then, Boris's voice broke the silence. "Hey, I'll give you a discount on that yellow coffin!" he called to us. "It's very comfortable. And super-fashionable. I'm telling you, a smart mouse would die to be buried in it! *Ha-ha-ha!*"

a smart mouse would die to be buried here!

The path wound around through the cemetery.

DUM-DUM-DEE-DUM!

Soon, we could no longer hear Boris. I was happy to be away from his awful jokes. Still, I wasn't thrilled about walking through a cemetery. A **thick fog** settled over us. It gave the whole place a ghostly glow. **MARBLE GRAVESTONES** sprang up from the earth. We passed an eerie stone tomb. Just then, Benjamin grabbed my jacket.

"Look, Uncle!" he squeaked, pointing to the tomb. "It's opening!"

I stared in horror as the marble slab covering the tomb began to rise.

I heard organ music.

Dum-dum-dee-dum-dum-dee-dum-dee-dum-dee-DUM!

The music filled the air. It was so loud. It was so sad. It was so SCARY. My paws were trembling so hard, I could barely stand. I had to use my tail for support. I felt like a mouse at an old age home. Break out the oxygen! I was about to FAINT.

Suddenly, Benjamin grabbed my paw. I snapped to attention. *No,* I scolded myself. This was no time for FAINTING. I had to think about my dear, sweet nephew. I couldn't leave the poor thing alone in this terrifying place. He could be scarred for life. He'd never visit another cemetery again. Even if yours truly kicked the bucket.

I pulled Benjamin back down the path. We had to get back to the funeral parlor. BUT THE FOG WAS TOO THICK.

I couldn't see the path anymore. Within minutes, I realized we were lost.

Just then, the organ music grew even louder. Dum-dum-dee-dum-dum-dee-dum-dee-dum-dee-DUM!

I looked up. The tomb was right in front of us again. And now it was wide open!

A mouselike snout appeared in the opening.

"Rancid rat hairs!" I screamed in terror.

"Keep your fur on. It's just me, Creepella von Cacklefur," a little voice answered. "Now, come inside. It's cold out there!"

A mouselike snout appeared in the opening.

CREEPELLA VON CACKLEFUR

We followed Creepella into the tomb. I studied her as we walked.

She had SHINY BLACK FUR and eyes as green as lima beans. Her long purple gown swirled around her as she moved. She wore matching purple pawnail polish. A **half–moon–shaped charm** hung from a chain around her neck. It was a strange look. But I had to admit, there was something attractive about Creepella. Maybe it was the way she moved. She barely made a sound. Or maybe it was her fur. It looked as soft as my favorite cat-fur rug.

When we reached Creepella's room, I

She wore a half-moon-shaped charm around her neck.

looked around. A **marble coffin** sat on the middle of the floor. It was made up with black satin sheets. I gulped. Creepella slept in a coffin? *How very odd.*

Next to the coffin was a black night table. A silver urn sat on the table. It was filled with a bouquet of dead flowers. Cobwebs hung down from the ceiling. The room was lit by a dirty oil lamp in the shape of a skull. I wrinkled my nose. I hate dirt. Creepella really needed a good mousecleaner. Maybe I could give her the name and number of my mousecleaner. There was no one better than Samantha Squeaky Clean. When she cleaned my mouse hole, it gleamed. I could eat

Creepella von Cacklefur

a five-course cheese dinner off the floor!

Now I stared at Creepella's **dingy walls**. Scary paintings were plastered all around. I saw a picture of a terrifying vampire. A snapshot of a GHOSTLY LOOKING CEMETERY hung below it. A mummy sculpture with red eyes glared down at me from a shelf. What a scary room!

Then I spotted the bookcase. Well, at least Creepella liked to read. After all, what's a mouse house without books? Books can take you on the most amazing adventures. And sometimes they can make you laugh your tail off.

I glanced at the titles on Creepella's shelf.

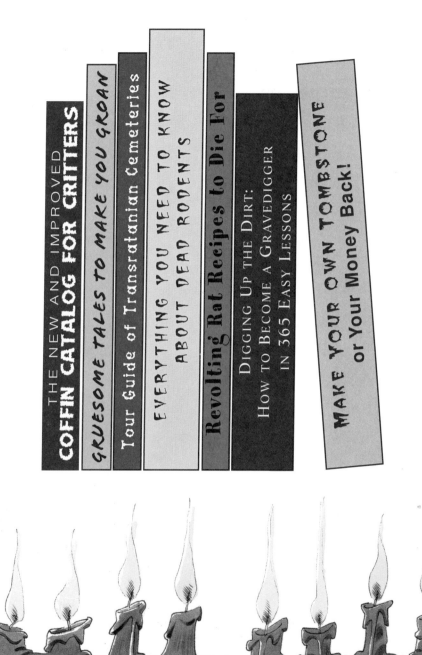

THE NEW AND IMPROVED
COFFIN CATALOG FOR CRITTERS

GRUESOME TALES TO MAKE YOU GROAN

Tour Guide of Transratanian Cemeteries

EVERYTHING YOU NEED TO KNOW
ABOUT DEAD RODENTS

Revolting Rat Recipes to Die For

DIGGING UP THE DIRT:
HOW TO BECOME A GRAVEDIGGER
IN 365 EASY LESSONS

MAKE YOUR OWN TOMBSTONE
or Your Money Back!

I CRINGED. Creepella sure seemed to like her daddy's business. I had never seen so many books about **DEATH** on one bookshelf. I turned around. Creepella was staring at us with a wicked smile. "So what can I do for you, **cutie mice**?" she asked in a soft voice.

I cleared my throat. Then I introduced Benjamin and myself. I explained that I was Pinky Pick's boss. And I told her about the **HALLOWEEN** book I was writing.

The whole time I was talking, Creepella stared at me. In fact, she never took her eyes off me. When I was done, she winked. THEN SHE MADE HER LIPS

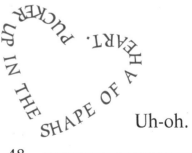

PUCKER UP IN THE SHAPE OF A HEART.

Uh-oh.

Benjamin grabbed my paw. "I think Creepella has a CRUSH on you, Uncle," he whispered.

I chewed my whiskers. Yes, Creepella was cute. And she seemed smart. But she was also **CREEPY**. And I mean creepy with a capital "**C**"!

YOU'RE AS PRECIOUS AS A CHEDDAR CHEESE PUFF!

Creepella opened her closet. She gave us some ideas for Halloween costumes. Benjamin took notes. She showed us her special scary makeup. She pulled out some horrifying wigs. Then she reached over and tickled my chin. "You have **gorgeous fur**, Geronimo," she crooned. "Has anyone ever told you you're as precious as a cheddar cheese puff?"

You cheddar cheese puff...

I broke out in a sweat. Don't get me wrong, I love female mice. But Creepella was just too creepy for me. Where would we go on a date? The CAT CEMETERY? "Um, well, I ..." I began.

Creepella cut me off. "Hey, I have a great idea!" she squeaked. "We'll have a HALLOWEEN PARTY here at my crypt!"

Benjamin was all for it. I wasn't surprised. What little mouse doesn't like a PARTY? "Yippee!" he cried, waving his tail in the air.

I wasn't half as excited. A party at Creepella's? I was creeped out just thinking about it! But I couldn't tell Benjamin. He would be so disappointed. "G-G-Great idea," I stammered instead.

In the meantime, Creepella was already busy making plans. "Let's see. We'll definitely need some special party food," she said.

With that, she punched a button on the wall. An enormous skull on her desk opened with a whir. Inside sat a funky new computer complete with a webcam.

Creepella giggled. "Thanks, Skully," she said, then she began to surf the Web.

After a while, a rodent's face appeared on the screen. It was Saucy Le Paws. He was the most popular chef in New Mouse City.

"Good eeeeevening, Creepella, darling," he said in his funny accent. "What eez it you weeesh for me to do?"

Creepella batted her eyelashes. "Oh, Saucy, I was wondering if you could make some food for my horrifying HALLOWEEN party," she asked.

Saucy curled his waxed whiskers. "So sorry, my sweeeeet," he said with a sigh. "I'm about to leeeeave for the Hamster Islands. It eeez the annual Cheese Ball Bake-off."

Creepella said good-bye to Saucy. I could tell she was disappointed.

Just then, Benjamin jumped to his paws. "I have an idea!" he shouted. "Let's ask *Tina* for advice!"

TINA SPICYTAIL

Tina Spicytail is my grandfather's cook and housekeeper. She is a tough old mouse who runs a tight kitchen. She's all business. Tina gets along fabumously with my grandfather **William Shortpaws**. Grandfather is all business himself. In fact, he's the founder of my paper, *The Rodent's Gazette*.

GRANDFATHER WILLIAM

SHORTPAWS

HELLO! HELLO! IT'S TINA!

I called Tina.

"Hello! Hello! Who's calling?" she yelled in a squeaky voice.

I told her it was me. Then I began to explain about Creepella's HALLOWEEN party.

"Allohwean?" Tina repeated. "What is it?"

I did my best to describe the holiday. I squeaked on and on about costumes and trick-or-treating. Finally, I told her we needed someone to cook a special Halloween meal. It needed to look scary but taste yummy.

When I was finished, Tina did not say a word. I coughed. Maybe she thought the whole idea was silly. Tina was a very **traditional** mouse.

"Um, it's OK if you are too busy," I mumbled. "I can call another cook."

Tina snorted. "Too busy?" she shrieked. "I am never too busy to cook. You name it, I can make it!"

Meanwhile, Creepella had begun printing out a menu. She slipped it to me. It was filled with gross-sounding dishes.

I read them to Tina. Once again, there was silence on the line.

"Um, so what do you think?" I murmured. "Can you do it, Tina?"

Another snort. "Of course I can do it!" she shouted. "Nothing is too hard for

SCARY MENU

HORS D'OEUVRES
Bats' Eyes on a Stick
Skeleton Fingers

MAIN COURSE
Slippery Sewer Slugs
Toad Meatballs in Vampire Sauce

DESSERT
Ghostly Goody Goop

DRINKS
Red Termite Blood
Sewer Water

Tina Spicytail! I'm going right away to find some **sewer slugs**. Then I will head off to the cemetery. Maybe I can catch a few bats there. . . ."

I gasped. *Uhhh-ohhh!*

Tina thought the dishes were real.

I did my best to set things straight. "Sewer slugs are really just penne pasta. Bats' eyes are actually cherry tomatoes. It's all just make-believe," I explained.

But I wasn't sure if Tina was listening. I heard pots and pans banging on the other end. "Tina will cook exactly what you ask for!" she insisted. "Now I must go. There's much work to be done!"

KISS! KISS!

I started to thank Tina, but she had already hung up. I put down the phone with a sigh. That's when I noticed Creepella. She was watching my every move. "**So tell me**, Geronimo," she squeaked in a soft voice. "Did I help you with your research? Are you ready to write your book?"

I nodded, feeling nervous. Creepella was staring at me as if I were a toasty cheese pancake.

I headed for the door. In a flash, Creepella leaped ahead of me. She held her paws out, blocking the door. Then she pursed her lips.

"Oh, no, my little cheese puff!" she cried. "You can't leave without giving me a kiss!" Then she began to chant, "Kiss! Kiss! Kiss! Kiss!

Kiss! Kiss! Kiss! Kiss!

My fur turned three shades of red. But I gave Creepella a quick peck on the snout. What could I do? She wouldn't let me go.

Creepella shrieked, clapping her paws. "Oh, Geronimo, you're such a dream!" she crooned. Then she demanded to know if I was dating **anyone special**.

I turned purple. What a nightmare! I didn't want to spend any more time with Creepella. She was way too scary. This was worse than walking through a cat cemetery at midnight.

Creepella winked at Benjamin. Then she began whispering loudly in his ear. "You will tell me if your uncle has any admirers, **OK**?" she began. "I want to know who they are. I want to know where they live. Then I will *scratch their eyes* out!"

I tried to stammer a reply, but Creepella wasn't even listening.

Benjamin and I both gasped. But Creepella just wiggled her long nails and laughed.

Suddenly, something brushed against my ear. I looked up just in time to see an ugly black bat.

"Moldy mozzarella!" I screamed.

Creepella scratched the bat's ear. "**By the way**, this is **Bitewing**," she said. "He's my pet bat."

61

I WILL GIVE YOU A RIDE HOME

I looked at my watch. I couldn't believe my eyes. It was dawn. We had spent the whole night in Creepella's crypt!

Creepella stretched. "Time to hit the **coffin**!" she announced, patting her strange bed. "I like to go to sleep at dawn and get up at sunset. But first, I will give you a ride home."

I tried to say no, but Creepella insisted. Before I knew it, we were sitting in a dark hearse. "This is my father's latest model, *The Roaring Bat*," she said, patting the dashboard. "It has a state-of-the-art satellite system with maps of all the cemeteries of the world."

She showed me a picture of the Regal Rodent Burial Ground. It is the most popular cemetery in New Mouse City. All of the **FAMOUSE RODENTS** are buried there.

Then Creepella hit the gas. Tires squealed as we peeled out of the cemetery. It was then that I realized who Creepella reminded me of. She was just like my sister, Thea. Both were absolutely horrifying drivers! I clutched my seat belt for dear life. Luckily, at dawn, the streets of New Mouse City are practically empty. Creepella ran **EVERY** red light. She went down **EACH** and **EVERY** one-way street the wrong way. And she rode up **ALL** of the curbs.

BORIS VON CACKLEFUR'S LATEST MODEL HEARSE

The Roaring Bat

MAP OF THE REGAL RODENT BURIAL GROUND OF NEW MOUSE CITY

1. The inventor
Alexander Graham Rat

2. The explorer
Christopher Columouse

3. The poet
Henry Wadsworth
Longfurrow

4. The playwright
William Shakespearat

5. The dancer
Paws Fosse

6. The singer
Squeaks Sinatrat

7. The scientist
Alfrat Einstein

8. The architect
Frank Lloyd Rat

9. The painter
Salvador Furry

10. The composer
Ratwig van Beethoven

At last, we came to a stop. I opened my eyes. Thank goodness, we had made it to the office. We were at *The Rodent's Gazette* at 17 SWISS CHEESE CENTER.

Benjamin and I tumbled out of the car.

I was white as a ghost!

"See you at the HALLOWEEN party!" Creepella said. She reached out and tickled my chin with her long nails. "And remember, you will dance only with me!" she added. Then, with a wild laugh, she ROARED off.

I'M A POLITE MOUSE

Benjamin and I scampered up the stairs to my office. I turned on the computer. Benjamin organized his notes. Then I began to write **FURIOUSLY**. Time was running out. I had to finish the book by tonight.

Five minutes later, Thea PHONED. She wanted to find out if I was done writing.

I wanted to squeak. I wanted to scream. I

squeak!!!

wanted to exclaim at the top of my lungs, "I'M A MOUSE, NOT A MACHINE!" But I held myself back. After all, I'm a polite mouse.

Ten minutes later, Trap PHONED. He told me we should put his photograph in the book.

I wanted to squeak. I wanted to scream. I wanted to tell him that no one would want to buy a book with his rotten picture in it. But I held myself back. After all, I'm a considerate mouse.

Fifteen minutes later, Creepella PHONED. At first, I couldn't understand a word she said. Then I realized she wasn't talking. She was blowing kisses at me. I wanted to squeak. I wanted to scream. I wanted to tell her that she was the creepiest mouse

I had ever met. But I didn't. After all, I'm a sensitive mouse.

Twenty minutes later, Tina PHONED, followed by Pinky Pick. I wanted to squeak. I wanted scream. I wanted to tell them I didn't have time for their ridiculous problems. But I held back. After all, I'm a responsible mouse.

Thirty minutes later, Thea PHONED again. She asked me once more if I had finished. This time, even though I am a polite, considerate, sensitive, responsible mouse, I couldn't hold back. I told her exactly what I was thinking.

She was so offended, she hung up on me!

Benjamin and I unplugged the phone. At last, we could work in peace.

We worked and worked and worked until . . .

I typed the last sentence.

At that very moment, Thea stormed into my office. "That's it!" she declared. "Time is up!"

Benjamin jumped up and down.

"Uncle, you are the greatest!"

he announced.

I laughed. I didn't believe I could write a book in such a hurry. But I did it. Yes, I, *Geronimo Stilton*, had written a whole book in one day!

"THE LOVE TANGO FOR TAILS"

It was finally the night of October 31.

Tina had decided that she could not cook in a strange kitchen. She would make everything at Grandfather's place. Then we would bring it to Creepella's. I wasn't about to argue with Tina. When she's cooking, she can be a total terror.

She stood in front of the stove, waving a silver rolling pin. She was barking out orders left and right. Her assistants raced around like hamsters caught on treadmills. Still, nothing was fast enough for Tina.

"You there! Bring me that soupspoon!" she screamed at a cowering rodent. "Yes, I'm talking to you, you cheddarbrain! MOVE

"I'm talking to you, cheddarbrain!"

IT, MOVE IT, MOVE IT!"

At eight o'clock, Tina laid down her rolling pin. "I am finished!" she announced. "Take it away!"

We packed up the food and brought it to Creepella's.

At nine o'clock, the guests started to arrive. There were lots of scary costumes. I saw someone dressed as a gravestone.

Another guest was wrapped up like a mummy. There were **WITCHES**, **GHOSTS**, **VAMPIRES**, and **GOBLINS**. I had to keep reminding myself they were just rodents. Everyone looked so real.

Then the band started to play "**THe Love Tango For TaiLs**." Mice whirled around the dance floor.

Just at that moment, I heard a voice

calling my name. Oh, no! It was Creepella.

Before I could stop her, she grabbed my paw. She dragged me onto the dance floor. Soon, she was spinning me around and around. I felt dizzy. Dizzy with fear!

Meanwhile, Creepella was whispering in my ear. "When will we see each other again, my Cheesy Puff?" she murmured.

"Never" sounded like a good time to me. But I didn't say a word. Instead, I steered her toward the buffet table. "I'm hungry," I squeaked. I stuffed a forkful of SEWER SLUGS into my mouth. I must say, they were delicious.

Next to the buffet table stood Creepella's father, Boris. "I never saw such a DISTURBING menu," he said with a smile. "It's so terribly GLOOMY, so horribly frightening. What artist cooked this masterpiece?"

I pointed to Tina. Boris bowed in front of her. "May I introduce myself?" he said. "I am **Boris von Cacklefur**. And you are . . . ?"

Tina looked Boris up and down. "I am *Tina Spicytail*," she replied. They shook paws. The next thing I knew, they were dancing up a storm. They seemed to have eyes only for each other. They were like *two lovebirds*.

Who would think two mice could fall in love on a scary holiday like Halloween?

May I have this dance?

I Absolutely Have to Go to the Dentist

The **Party** continued late into the night. More dancing. More eating. *Where did these rodents get all their energy?* I wondered. I was so tired, I could barely stand on my paws.

My head was pounding from the loud music. I stood in a corner of the room, staring at the clock. I know I sound like a party poopmouse, but I was beat!

Finally, at five o'clock in the morning, the party ended.

I spotted Boris and Tina strolling through the cemetery paw in paw. "What a *charming* backyard," Tina commented.

Boris nodded. He gazed lovingly at the many tombstones. "My clients tell me it's to die for," he snickered.

The two mice burst out in peals of laughter. Then they climbed into Boris's black hearse. "Bye-bye, Geronimo!" Tina yelled out the window. "Boris and I are going on a little vacation to **Transratania**!"

I gulped. Transratania is a very spooky place. Some believe it's crawling with vampires.

Just then, Creepella appeared at my side. She batted her eyelashes at me. "Geronimo, I just had the most fabumouse idea!" she squeaked. "Why don't we go to **Transratania, too? I hear it's very romantic.**"

My fur broke out in a sweat. I did not want to go to Transratania with Creepella. I did not want to go anywhere with Creepella. But what could I say? She was so pushy. She was so demanding. She was so creepy. I chewed my whiskers, deep in thought. Meanwhile, Creepella put her paw around my shoulder. She was grinning like a CAT who has just swallowed a mouse. I stared at her little pointy teeth. That's when I got an idea. "Cheese niblets!" I squeaked. "I just remembered I have a very important appointment. Yes, I have an emergency dentist appointment. I must leave right away," I added.

Creepella patted my paw, concerned. "Oh, poor Cheesy Puff," she crooned. "Do you have a toothache?"

"No," I answered without thinking. Oops. I didn't mean to say that. I think it was her calling me Cheesy Puff again that threw me.

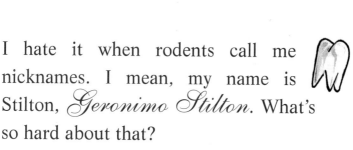

I hate it when rodents call me nicknames. I mean, my name is Stilton, *Geronimo Stilton*. What's so hard about that?

I turned to Creepella. I told her the dentist needed to do an emergency cleaning.

"At five o'clock in the morning?" Creepella asked.

I nodded. After all, a mouse's health is nothing to squeak about. I gave her a quick hug. Then I jumped in a taxi and left.

Back home, I triple-locked my door. I breathed a big sigh of relief. It felt so good to be home. Away from the party. Away from the cemetery. Away from Creepella. I crawled into my bed and pulled the covers up to my snout. Ah, alone at last.

At that moment, the phone r a n g.

I looked at it. What if it was her? What if

it was that creepy mouse? Oh, why couldn't she leave me alone?

Ring, ring. Ring, ring!

I couldn't take it anymore. "Stilton speaking, *Geronimo Stilton*!"

I barked into the phone.

Stilton speaking, Geronimo Stilton!

But it wasn't Creepella. It was my sales manager, Shif T. Paws.

"Geronimo! The book!!! It's on the list!" he shouted.

I was so tired I couldn't think straight.

"What list? What book?" I mumbled.

Shif laughed. "Your book! Your HALLOWEEN book!" he squeaked. "It's on the top of the bestseller list! We're gonna be rich!"

80

Rich? I grinned. Maybe HALLOWEEN isn't such a bad holiday after all, I decided. I mean, it's not all about being SCARED out of your fur. It's also about doing things with your friends and family. Thea and I always had fun carving out pumpkins when we were young mice. And Trap used to help me with my costume. One time, I dressed up as a MUMMY. One time, I was a GHOST. And once, I even went as a giant book. Now, that was one good story!

Geronimooooo!!!

Hey, Mouse Friends,

Here's a book I bet you'd like to read. It's the book I was just talking about, my HALLOWEEN bestseller. Hope you like it!

Cheesy good wishes!

Your rodent friend,

Geronimo Stilton

HALLOWEEN!!!

What a SCREAM!
Read on and you will find
Some tips to mastermind
An absolutely TERRIFYING,
HORRIFYING, SCARIFYING

HALLOWEEN PARTY!

The True Story of Halloween

The Celts, who once lived in Ireland, celebrated the arrival of winter with a holiday called All Hallows Eve. They lit fires and danced around them. They wore frightening masks to scare away ghosts. They carved pumpkins and placed candles inside of them. According to legend, the candlelight was thought to keep away spirits of the night.

Today we call this holiday Halloween. It is celebrated on October 31. Young rodents dress up in costumes and go from mouse hole to mouse hole squeaking, "Trick or treat!" They are then rewarded with all different kinds of cheesy-good candy treats. Yum!

GAMES

Scary Movie Squeakfest

Start with a group of friends. One rodent leaves the room. The others divide into two teams. Each team comes up with the title of a scary movie. The rodent returns to the room. Each team begins to act out their movie title. The rodent tries to guess the names of the movies. The first team to make him understand their title wins.

Left Paw Poet

The player who writes this phrase the fastest wins. But she must write it with her left paw.

Ratty the rat wore a cat-fur hat.

Vampire Alphabet

Squeak your ABC's backward. The player who makes no mistakes is the winner.

The Speedy Spider

Set a timer for one minute. Now try drawing a spider in a web before the minute is up. (Cheese niblets! It's not as easy as it sounds!)

The Touchy Witch

Turn off all the lights in a room. Put on some scary background music. Make all of your guests sit in a circle. Place the objects in bowls, then pass them around the room. As each object is passed, you chant:

▶ Touch the witch's **teeth.**
(candy corn)

▶ Touch the witch's **ears.**
(dried apricots)

▶ Touch the witch's **eyes.**
(peeled grapes)

▶ Touch the witch's **nails.**
(pumpkin seeds)

▶ Touch the witch's **spit.**
(yogurt)

▶ Touch the witch's **hair.**
(twine)

▶ Touch the witch's **brains.**
(cooked spaghetti)

Before the game begins, ask a friend to hide outside the door. At the end of the game, that person should shriek, "Ooooh! I'm the witch!"

OOOOOOH! I'M THE WITCH!

Spooky Puppet Theater

1. Cut some scary shapes out of cardboard (for example, ghost, goblin, vampire, bat, pumpkin).

Make sure you are using safety scissors.

2. Tape a wooden stick to the back of each shape.

3. Turn off the lights in the room. Have your guests face a bare wall. Shine a flashlight at the wall. Move each shape in front of the flashlight to make a shadow on the wall.
Then tell a scary story using the shapes.

DECORATIONS
Jack-o'-lantern

1. Ask an adult to cut off the top of a ripe pumpkin.

2. Using a spoon, scoop out all the pulp from the pumpkin.

3. With a felt-tip pen, draw a nose, eyes, and mouth on the pumpkin.

Warning: Make sure an adult helps you, because knives can be very dangerous!

Depending on the designs, your pumpkins can have many different expressions.

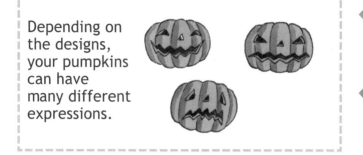

4. Ask an adult to cut out the nose, eyes, and mouth with a carving knife.

5. Put a candle inside the pumpkin. Have an adult light it. Put your pumpkin in the window.

Warning: Make sure an adult helps you! Matches are dangerous. <u>Never</u> leave a flame unattended.

How to Make a Terrifying Table

1. Instead of a tablecloth, place black crepe paper on the table.

2. Attach the paper to the table using double-sided tape.

3. Don't forget the corners!

4. Decorate the table with orange bows and cutout orange cardboard shapes of vampires, pumpkins, and witches.

5. Ask an adult to light a jack-o'-lantern. Then have him put it on a plate and place it in the middle of the table.

Warning: **Never** leave the flame unattended.

Be sure to use safety scissors.

COSTUMES
Mummy

You will need: several rolls of toilet paper, a white T-shirt, and white shorts or tights.

1. Put on a white T-shirt and white shorts or tights.

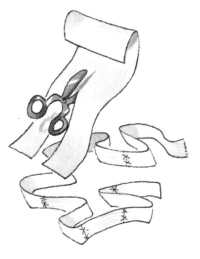

2. Starting at your ankles, begin wrapping the toilet paper around your body.

3. Continue wrapping the toilet paper until you reach the top of your head.

Leave space for your mouth, nose, and eyes.

Be careful. Use safety scissors. Ask an adult to help you wrap yourself up.

Witch

You will need: purple or black lipstick, black eye pencil, red lip pencil, black nail polish or fake fingernails, a pointed witch's hat, a dark dress, black tights, black shoes, a thick book, aluminum foil, and a broom.

1. Using the black eye pencil, make your eyebrows thick. Then draw wrinkles around your eyes and nose.

2. With the red lip pencil, draw a red line under your eyes. Then carefully put on the lipstick, the nail polish or fake fingernails, and the dress, tights, shoes, and hat.

3. Cover the book with aluminum foil. This is your book of magic spells.

Hint:
For extra-spookiness, glue some silver powder onto your broom's handle.

4. Don't forget your broom!

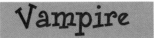

Vampire

You will need: white face makeup, black eye pencil, red lip pencil, black lipstick, purple or black nail polish, dark pants, a white shirt, a black vest, a long black cape, black socks, and black shoes.

1. Put the white face makeup all over your face. Using the black eye pencil, draw a triangle on your forehead, your cheeks, and your chin, then color in the triangles.

2. Draw in thick arched eyebrows. Outline your upper eyelid in black pencil. Draw a red line under your lower lashes. Put the black lipstick on your lips and the purple or black nail polish on your nails. Using the red lip pencil, draw a drop of blood near the corner of your mouth.

Hint: You can also put on fake vampire teeth or carry a little bottle of red liquid that looks like blood.

Skeleton

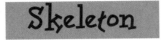

You will need: black tights, a black T-shirt, black gloves, white chalk or white fabric paint, and a black eye pencil.

1. Using the white fabric paint or chalk, draw bones on the tights and T-shirt. Ask an adult to help you.

2. Paint the front and back of the skeleton. Wait until the paint is dry before putting on the costume.

3. Now it's time to paint your face. Using the black eye pencil, draw circles around each eye. Draw a triangle above each nostril.

4. Outline your lips in black pencil.

Hint: Carry a rubber bone or a glow-in-the-dark skull. If you have long hair, hide it under a tight-fitting white cap.

Frankenstein

You will need: green face makeup, a black eye pencil, purple or black lipstick, black nail polish, hair gel, a T-shirt, black pants, a black suit jacket, and black or brown boots.

1. Apply the green face makeup all over your face. Using the black eye pencil, outline your eyes. Then draw scars on your forehead and on one of your cheeks. Put on lipstick and nail polish.

2. Use the hair gel to paste down your hair.

3. Put on the T-shirt, pants, jacket, and boots.

Hint: Walk like a monster! Take stiff, jerky steps.

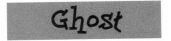
Ghost

You will need: an old white sheet, a black felt-tip pen, white socks, white gloves, and a ball of black yarn.

1. Cut the sheet into a circle.

2. For the eyes, cut out two holes in the middle of the circle. Draw a circle around each eyehole.

3. Put on the white socks and gloves.

4. Tie the black yarn so it doesn't unravel. Make sure to leave a long strand—perhaps two feet long—loose. Tie the loose strand around your ankle. Hooray! Now you have a ball and chain.

Be careful. Use safety scissors.

SCARY MENU

for..................'s party

on...........................

HORS D'OEUVRES
Bats' Eyes on a Stick
Skeleton Fingers

MAIN COURSE
Slippery Sewer Slugs
Toad Meatballs in Vampire Sauce

DESSERT
Ghostly Goody Goop

DRINKS
Red Termite Blood
Sewer Water

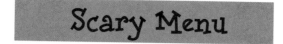

Scary Menu

Remember the menu on page 56? Make a copy of the menu on the facing page and write in your name and the date of your party. You can also make copies of the place card on this page so there is one for each of your friends. Then follow the recipes for cooking these funny dishes. You will need the help of a grown-up. Cooking can be dangerous — especially when the menu is so gross!

PLACE CARD

Bats' Eyes on a Stick

You will need: cherry tomatoes and toothpicks.

1. Take some cherry tomatoes and insert a toothpick into each.

2. Place them in a black bowl for a spooky look.

Skeleton Fingers

You will need: one bag of mini pretzel sticks.

Slippery Sewer Slugs

For four people, you will need: one 16-ounce box of penne pasta, 1/4 teaspoon oil, and 1/8 teaspoon salt.

1. Place a pot of water on stovetop.

2. Put in oil and salt.

3. Bring water to a boil.

4. Add pasta to boiling water.

5. Reduce heat. Let simmer until pasta is cooked.

Toad Meatballs in Vampire Sauce

For four people, you will need: one 16-ounce jar of seasoned tomato sauce, one pound ground beef, one small chopped onion, 1/4 cup milk,

1/2 cup dry bread crumbs, one egg, a pinch of garlic, and salt and pepper.

1. Mix all the ingredients together, except for the sauce. Shape the meat into balls.

2. Arrange the meatballs in a baking pan. Bake uncovered in 400°F oven until done (about 20 to 25 minutes).

3. Put tomato sauce in saucepan. Bring to a simmer. When meatballs are cooked, add to sauce. Cook meatballs in sauce for another 5 to 10 minutes. You can also serve the sauce with the Slippery Sewer Slugs.

MeooowWWWWWWWWWWWW!!!

Ghostly Goody Goop

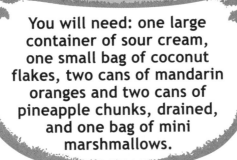

You will need: one large container of sour cream, one small bag of coconut flakes, two cans of mandarin oranges and two cans of pineapple chunks, drained, and one bag of mini marshmallows.

Mix all ingredients together and refrigerate. Serve chilled.

Red Termite Blood

You will need: red fruit punch.

Sewer Water

You will need: one bottle of mineral water and one bottle of club soda.

mineral water

club soda

ABOUT THE AUTHOR

Born in New Mouse City, Mouse Island, Geronimo Stilton is Rattus Emeritus of Mousomorphic Literature and of Neo-Ratonic Comparative Philosophy. For the past twenty years, he has been running *The Rodent's Gazette*, New Mouse City's most widely read daily newspaper.

Stilton was awarded the Ratitzer Prize for his scoop on *The Curse of the Cheese Pyramid*. He has also received the Andersen 2000 Prize for Personality of the Year. One of his best-sellers won the 2002 eBook Award for world's best ratlings' electronic book. His works have been published all over the globe.

In his spare time, Mr. Stilton collects antique cheese rinds and plays golf. But what he most enjoys is telling stories to his nephew Benjamin.

Don't miss any of my other fabumouse adventures!

#1 Lost Treasure of the Emerald Eye
#2 The Curse of the Cheese Pyramid
#3 Cat and Mouse in a Haunted House
#4 I'm Too Fond of My Fur!
#5 Four Mice Deep in the Jungle
#6 Paws Off, Cheddarface!
#7 Red Pizzas for a Blue Count
#8 Attack of the Bandit Cats
#9 A Fabumouse Vacation for Geronimo
#10 All Because of a Cup of Coffee
#11 It's Halloween, You 'Fraidy Mouse!
#12 Merry Christmas, Geronimo!
#13 The Phantom of the Subway
#14 The Temple of the Ruby of Fire
#15 The Mona Mousa Code
#16 A Cheese-Colored Camper
#17 Watch Your Whiskers, Stilton!
#18 Shipwreck on the Pirate Islands
#19 My Name is Stilton, Geronimo Stilton
#20 Surf's Up, Geronimo!
#21 The Wild, Wild West
#22 The Secret of Cacklefur Castle
#23 Valentine's Day Disaster
#24 Field Trip to Niagara Falls

#25 The Search for Sunken Treasure
#26 The Mummy With No Name
#27 The Christmas Toy Factory
#28 Wedding Crasher
#29 Down and Out Down Under
#30 The Mouse Island Marathon
#31 The Mysterious Cheese Thief
#32 Valley of the Giant Skeletons
#33 Geronimo and the Gold Medal Mystery
#34 Geronimo Stilton, Secret Agent
#35 A Very Merry Christmas
#36 Geronimo's Valentine
#37 The Race Across America
#38 A Fabumouse School Adventure
#39 Singing Sensation
#40 The Karate Mouse
#41 Mighty Mount Kilimanjaro
#42 The Peculiar Pumpkin Thief
#43 I'm Not a Supermouse!
#44 The Giant Diamond Robbery
#45 The Haunted Castle
A Christmas Tale
Christmas Catastrophe

Be sure to check out these very special editions!

THE KINGDOM OF FANTASY

THE QUEST FOR PARADISE: THE RETURN TO THE KINGDOM OF FANTASY

And look for this new series about my friend Creepella von Cacklefur!

#1 THE THIRTEEN GHOSTS

#2 MEET ME IN HORRORWOOD

If you like my brother's books, you'll love mine!

THEA STILTON
AND THE
DRAGON'S CODE

THEA STILTON
AND THE
MOUNTAIN OF FIRE

THEA STILTON
AND THE GHOST OF
THE SHIPWRECK

THEA STILTON
AND THE
SECRET CITY

THEA STILTON
AND THE MYSTERY
IN PARIS

THEA STILTON
AND THE CHERRY
BLOSSOM ADVENTURE

THEA STILTON
AND THE
STAR CASTAWAYS

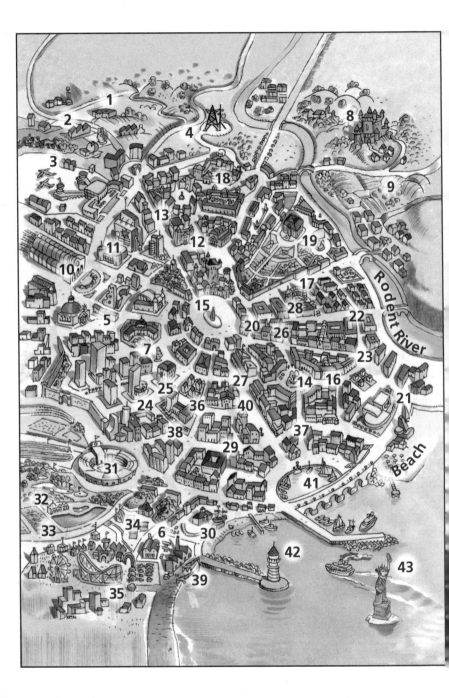

Map of New Mouse City

1. Industrial Zone
2. Cheese Factories
3. Angorat International Airport
4. WRAT Radio and Television Station
5. Cheese Market
6. Fish Market
7. Town Hall
8. Snotnose Castle
9. The Seven Hills of Mouse Island
10. Mouse Central Station
11. Trade Center
12. Movie Theater
13. Gym
14. Catnegie Hall
15. Singing Stone Plaza
16. The Gouda Theater
17. Grand Hotel
18. Mouse General Hospital
19. Botanical Gardens
20. Cheap Junk for Less (Trap's store)
21. Parking Lot
22. Mouseum of Modern Art
23. University and Library
24. *The Daily Rat*
25. *The Rodent's Gazette*
26. Trap's House
27. Fashion District
28. The Mouse House Restaurant
29. Environmental Protection Center
30. Harbor Office
31. Mousidon Square Garden
32. Golf Course
33. Swimming Pool
34. Blushing Meadow Tennis Courts
35. Curlyfur Island Amusement Park
36. Geronimo's House
37. New Mouse City Historic District
38. Public Library
39. Shipyard
40. Thea's House
41. New Mouse Harbor
42. Luna Lighthouse
43. The Statue of Liberty

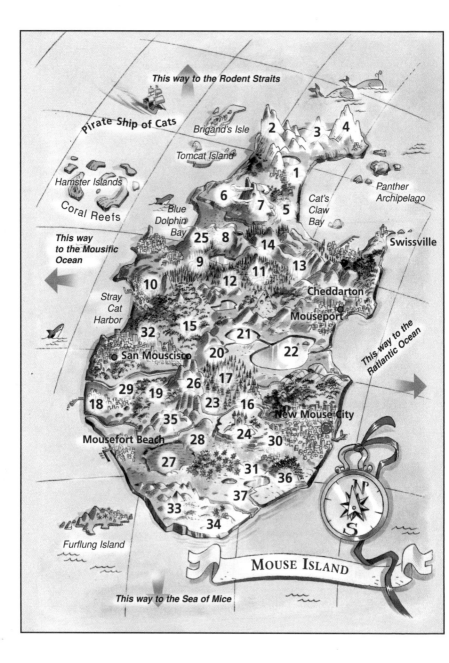

Map of Mouse Island

<table>
<tr><td>1.</td><td>Big Ice Lake</td><td>21.</td><td>Lake Lake Lake</td></tr>
<tr><td>2.</td><td>Frozen Fur Peak</td><td>22.</td><td>Lake Lakelakelake</td></tr>
<tr><td>3.</td><td>Slipperyslopes Glacier</td><td>23.</td><td>Cheddar Crag</td></tr>
<tr><td>4.</td><td>Coldcreeps Peak</td><td>24.</td><td>Cannycat Castle</td></tr>
<tr><td>5.</td><td>Ratzikistan</td><td>25.</td><td>Valley of the Giant Sequoia</td></tr>
<tr><td>6.</td><td>Transratania</td><td></td><td></td></tr>
<tr><td>7.</td><td>Mount Vamp</td><td>26.</td><td>Cheddar Springs</td></tr>
<tr><td>8.</td><td>Roastedrat Volcano</td><td>27.</td><td>Sulfurous Swamp</td></tr>
<tr><td>9.</td><td>Brimstone Lake</td><td>28.</td><td>Old Reliable Geyser</td></tr>
<tr><td>10.</td><td>Poopedcat Pass</td><td>29.</td><td>Vole Vail</td></tr>
<tr><td>11.</td><td>Stinko Peak</td><td>30.</td><td>Ravingrat Ravine</td></tr>
<tr><td>12.</td><td>Dark Forest</td><td>31.</td><td>Gnat Marshes</td></tr>
<tr><td>13.</td><td>Vain Vampires Valley</td><td>32.</td><td>Munster Highlands</td></tr>
<tr><td>14.</td><td>Goose Bumps Gorge</td><td>33.</td><td>Mousehara Desert</td></tr>
<tr><td>15.</td><td>The Shadow Line Pass</td><td>34.</td><td>Oasis of the Sweaty Camel</td></tr>
<tr><td>16.</td><td>Penny Pincher Lodge</td><td></td><td></td></tr>
<tr><td>17.</td><td>Nature Reserve Park</td><td>35.</td><td>Cabbagehead Hill</td></tr>
<tr><td>18.</td><td>Las Ratayas Marinas</td><td>36.</td><td>Rattytrap Jungle</td></tr>
<tr><td>19.</td><td>Fossil Forest</td><td>37.</td><td>Rio Mosquito</td></tr>
<tr><td>20.</td><td>Lake Lake</td><td></td><td></td></tr>
</table>

Dear mouse friends,
Thanks for reading, and farewell
till the next book.
It'll be another whisker-licking-good
adventure, and that's a promise!

Geronimo Stilton